# MAMA'S WINDOW

## BY LYNN RUBRIGHT

### AFTERWORD BY PATRICIA C. McKISSACK

### ILLUSTRATIONS BY DUANE SMITH

LEE & LOW BOOKS Inc.
New York

LEE & LOW BOOKS Inc., 95 Madison Avenue, New York, NY 10016
leeandlow.com

Manufactured in the United States of America

Book design by Tania Garcia
Book production by The Kids at Our House

The text is set in Venetian

(HC) 10 9 8 7 6 5 4 3 2 1
(PB) 10 9 8 7 6 5 4 3
First Edition

Library of Congress Cataloging-in-Publication Data
Rubright, Lynn.
       Mama's window / by Lynn Rubright ; afterword by Patricia C. McKissack ;
illustrated by Duane Smith.— 1st ed.
             p. cm.
       Very loosely based on a childhood incident in the life of the Reverend Owen
Whitfield, an African American sharecropper and minister who was vice-president
of the integrated Southern Tenant Farmers' Union in Arkansas in the 1930s.
       Summary: His dying mother's insistence leads an eleven-year-old black child
to be raised by his disabled uncle, in the swamps of the Mississippi Delta in the
early 1900s, and to recall her tireless work to fund a stained glass window for her
church.
       ISBN 978-1-58430-160-8 (hc)    ISBN 978-1-60060-335-8 (pb)
       [1. Glass painting and staining—Fiction. 2. Church buildings—Fiction.
3. Grief—Fiction. 4. Orphans—Fiction. 5. Uncles—Fiction. 6. African
Americans—Fiction. 7. Mississippi River—History—20th century—Fiction.
8. Mississippi—History—20th century—Fiction.] I. Smith, Duane, ill. II. Title.
PZ7.R83137Mam 2005
[Fic]—dc22                                        2004023409

# MAMA'S WINDOW

To the memories of Reverend Owen H. Whitfield (1894–1965), sharecropper, preacher, and union organizer, and Fannie Cook (1893–1949), St. Louis novelist, artist, and social activist, whose inspirational writings about Reverend Whitfield led to the creation of Mama's Window.

And to Robert Rubright, my wonderfully supportive husband, who often took me to research the Mississippi Delta and offered his discerning notes on the manuscript.

—L.R.

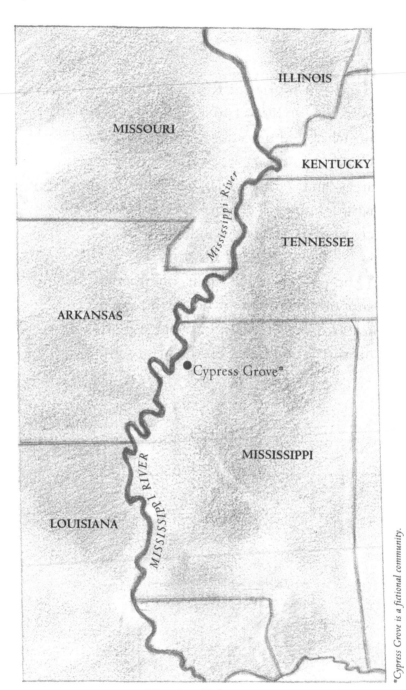

Mississippi Delta region

# Chapter One

The familiar aroma of hot water cornbread frying in bacon fat aroused Sugar from a deep sleep. He lay curled like a cat on the old iron cot.

Sugar stretched. Rusty bedsprings creaked.

"Time to get up, James Earle!" When he was irritated, Uncle Free always called Sugar by his proper name.

Sugar turned over and watched Uncle Free flipping cornbread patties in the fry pan. Uncle

Free's spine was crooked, one leg was shorter than the other, and one arm hung weakly at his side. He had been hurt in a train wreck, working as a porter on the railroad out of Memphis.

*A cripple*, thought Sugar. *Uncle Free ain't nothin' but a cripple.* Immediately he was ashamed, hearing his mama's voice say "He's a lucky man to be alive, Sugar."

Sugar buried his face in Mama's crazy quilt that still smelled of their old cabin. Since Mama died of heart trouble six months ago, Sugar had been staying with his uncle, who lived in a one-room shack at the edge of a swamp in the Mississippi Delta.

Sugar had no other choice. He was an orphan now, and his mama, Ida Mae Martin, had made it known before she died that Sugar was to live with her brother in the swamp. Sugar knew Uncle Free didn't have anything to say about it either. When Ida Mae made up her mind about something, that was that.

Lifting his head, Sugar noticed Uncle Free had set the wobbly table with two chipped plates and cups. Nets, bamboo fishing poles, hooks, and lines hung on the weather-beaten wall that framed the single smoky glass window.

Through the window Sugar watched the early summer morning mist rise from the swamp amid tall, shadowy cypress trees. Little knobby knees jutted out of the water around the splayed trunks of the trees. Their roots reached like wooden tentacles down into the black water. *Those trees ready to snatch me from the boat every time we go fishin'*, Sugar thought.

The water terrified Sugar. The rickety dock, slippery with fish guts, stretched into the swamp on stilts. Sugar feared he would slip off the dock into a watery grave. Even though Uncle Free was giving him swimming lessons, Sugar didn't think he was a good enough swimmer to save himself if he fell into the water.

One time Sugar had stood in the oozing mud too long and leeches had attached themselves to his ankles and calves.

"Get these off me!" he had screamed.

Uncle Free had laughed as he plucked the slimy creatures from Sugar's legs. The leeches left little bloody bite marks.

"Ain't nothin' to be scared of, boy," Uncle Free had said. "Fancy doctors use leeches to bleed rich folks of their fevers. Here you gettin' treatment for free."

"But I ain't sick!" Sugar had yelled. "Get 'em off me, Uncle Free."

Sugar quickly learned to keep his feet off the soft bottom. He became an expert at treading water, wiggling his arms and legs fast enough to keep his head above the surface.

"You got yourself a good dog paddle, Sugar," said Uncle Free, chuckling. "Good enough to get you outta trouble if you end up in the water."

Sugar promised himself that would never happen. Oh how he hated the swamp, bayou, even Sun Lake, with their murky waters, snakes, and swarms of pesky mosquitoes. The never-ending racket of croaking bullfrogs rang constantly in his ears.

Sugar snuggled deeper under the quilt. It was pieced together from snippets of checked, plaid, and calico fabrics Mama had made their clothes from over the years. *Not Mama's quilt anymore,* thought Sugar. *It's mine now.*

Suddenly Uncle Free threw back the covers and nudged Sugar's shoulder.

"James Earle, I ain't gonna call you again," Uncle Free shouted.

Sugar looked into his uncle's grizzled face, one eye near blind. "Uh-huh," Sugar grunted.

He turned away and focused on the quilt. Its patterns and colors reminded Sugar of a stained glass window—the one that was going to be set behind the pulpit in the new Sweet Kingdom Church. Sugar's mama had worked for years to raise money for the window in the new church, and today was the groundbreaking for the building.

"James Earle, time to get up!" Uncle Free's voice meant business now. "You gotta eat and get to work."

Sugar dragged himself out of bed and slipped into his overalls. He shook out the quilt and spread it on the cot, like Mama had made him do every morning. Then he nudged an old stool up to the table with his foot and slid onto it.

While he picked at the crisp fried cornbread his uncle put before him, Sugar stole glances at the man who sat across the table. Sugar had heard the gossip: When the chickens stop laying, or the cow's milk curdles, or butter won't come, it must be old Free McBride putting a spell on them with his evil eye.

Of course Sugar knew better. "Don' you listen to that ugly conjure talk," Mama used to tell him. "Ain't none of it true, and you know it, Sugar."

When Uncle Free recovered from that terrible train wreck, he had come back to Cypress Grove to fish, catch turtles, and gig for frogs in the swamp. It was the only living left to him. Folks were mighty nice to Free to his face when he delivered fish, but behind his back they said nasty things.

Mama had told Sugar that after the accident Uncle Free got some money from his small life and disability insurance but that he never spent a penny of it. Uncle Free said no amount of money could ever put his body back right. As far as Sugar could see, Uncle Free had no need for that money. He got along just fine living off the chickens in the yard and what he caught in the water and grew in the little garden behind the shack.

The children who lived in Cypress Grove, especially Stewie Pearson, called Free McBride "that ol' swamp rat." Sugar had never told Mama how the other boys teased him for having an uncle who lived in the swamp.

"Eat up, boy," Uncle Free barked, swallowing the last of his coffee. "There's work to be done. Nets need mendin'. There's frogs to gig and fish to catch. And you gotta practice usin' one of the boats on your own."

"But it's Sunday," Sugar said sullenly. "Mama never washed and ironed on Sunday, and I didn' tote laundry to the people she worked for in Wilson City. Why we gotta fish?"

"'Cause you gotta eat on Sunday," Uncle Free snapped.

Sugar was silent as he cleared the dishes into the lead-lined sink with the pump hitched to one side. He rinsed the plates clean, dried them, and put them back on the shelf. Then as Uncle Free took a gigging hook off the wall and started toward the door, Sugar broke the silence.

"It's groundbreakin' day for the new church, Uncle Free," he mumbled. "Mama would've been there."

Uncle Free stopped and turned around.

"You wanna go to the church groundbreakin', James Earle? I ain't stoppin' you. Take the little boat. Time you go out on the water by yourself anyways."

"You be wantin' to come along, Uncle Free?" Sugar asked tentatively.

Uncle Free shook his head. "Naw," he said. "Gave up churchgoin' years ago. Church folks ain't my kinda folks."

# CHAPTER TWO

**A**fter breakfast Sugar walked across the porch and onto the narrow, weathered dock that stretched out into the black swamp water like a pointed finger.

*The finger of death*, thought Sugar, fear curling up inside him. He didn't much like the idea of going out alone. He saw himself getting tangled in weeds and drowning if the boat turned over, but he didn't dare say so.

Suddenly the dock shook as Uncle Free came up behind Sugar. The two small boats, looped by frayed ropes to a post, bobbed in the dark water.

"Better get goin' if you're goin'." Uncle Free untied the rope and pulled the smaller boat close. Sugar sat down on the edge of the dock and carefully eased himself into the wobbling boat.

"Jam the pole into the mud like I showed you," said Uncle Free. "Remember, use it to shove yourself forward. Pole's better than oars in shallow water. Oars get tangled in weeds and roots. Save your oars for open water in the bayou and Sun Lake."

Uncle Free paused, then added, "And don' forget to study on those cypress trees, boy. They spread out under the water and poke up like little woody beasts where you don' expect 'em. Easy to smash up against one and jab a hole in the boat."

This was more words than Sugar had heard Uncle Free say at one time in his life. *He so worried 'bout how I manage the boat,* Sugar thought, he should come with me. But Sugar didn't say anything. He just took the pole from Uncle Free's outstretched hand.

Sugar had been following his uncle in his

own boat every day, mirroring his maneuvers, but until now Sugar had never ventured into the swamp alone. Standing in the stern of the boat, Sugar checked his balance.

"Well, what you waitin' for, boy?" asked Uncle Free. "Get goin'. You gonna be late for the ceremony."

Jamming his pole into the murky water, Sugar shoved off. Rhythmically lifting and plunging the pole into the mud, he surged forward with each thrust. Soon he was out of sight of Uncle Free's shack.

One more long jab into the mud and Sugar swerved out of the dense swamp and into the bayou, a slow-moving path of water that opened into Sun Lake a hundred yards beyond. The cypress trees grew farther apart. Cottonwoods and willow trees lined the bank. The water was deeper now. The pole no longer reached bottom. It was time to row.

Sugar knelt down, slid the pole under the seat, and gingerly crawled to the middle of the boat. He turned around and sat facing the stern, bracing his legs for balance. He set the oars in the oarlocks.

Glancing over his shoulder, Sugar pulled first

on one oar, then the other. He rowed out of the bayou and into Sun Lake. Usually the lake was calm and easy to row across. Sugar had done it many times with Uncle Free sitting in the stern giving him directions. Still, Sugar heard his uncle's warnings in his head: "Beware the power of water, James Earle. There's tangles of mud, roots, and branches lurkin' below. They called snags. They can grab a boat, flip it over, and suck you under if you ain't careful."

Sugar took care to steer clear of the scrubby little spine of land in the middle of Sun Lake that everyone called "the island." Uncle Free gave Sugar his swimming lessons on the southern bank of the island since it was mostly clear of snakes and weeds.

Sugar rowed on toward Cypress Grove. When he reached shallow water, he switched back to using his pole. Beyond the great weeping willow tree on the bank of the cove, Sugar could see the Sweet Kingdom Church nestled near a cluster of cabins. People were already arriving for the groundbreaking ceremony.

The old wooden church was to be torn down and replaced with a new building. A wave of grief for Mama surged through Sugar, followed by a feeling of pride. It was Mama who had made sure the new church would have a colorful stained glass window with black angels going up a staircase to heaven.

Sugar maneuvered his boat under the cascade of arching willow fronds. He jumped into the water and shoved the little boat onto the muddy bank. The water felt good on his bare feet.

From under the branches of the willow tree, Sugar watched as members of the church set up folding chairs where the new building was going to stand. Then he slipped through the branches and started up the hill toward the congregation.

Sugar hadn't been to church since Mama's funeral. Uncle Free wasn't a churchgoing man, but he had attended Ida Mae's funeral to honor her memory. It was after the service that Sugar had overheard the church women gossiping. They whispered about his mama choosing Free McBride as his guardian rather than having him pass back and forth among the church members' families, like some orphans he knew.

Mrs. Pearson, Mama's best friend, spotted Sugar. She waved. "Sugar, honey, hurry up!" she called. "Ceremony's 'bout to begin. You come sit by me, ya hear?"

# CHAPTER THREE

Sugar could see Stewie Pearson standing with his daddy and the other men off to one side. Stewie and Sugar had never been friends, though their mamas had tried to make the boys like each other.

Mrs. Pearson got up from where she was sitting and engulfed Sugar in a big hug. She nodded to the seat next to her. Obediently, he sat down.

"You gettin' along all right, Sugar?" Mrs. Pearson asked.

"Yes, ma'am," he replied.

"I declare, I don' know what your mama was thinkin' of, lettin' you stay with that ol' fella in the swamp."

Sugar wasn't sure himself. He just wished that Mrs. Pearson would stop talking about Mama.

Mrs. Pearson craned her neck and saw her son hanging back near his daddy. "Stewie," she called. "You come over here and sit by Sugar too, ya hear?"

Stewie in his Sunday pressed pants, fresh shirt, and polished shoes ambled over to where Sugar sat. "Look at him, Mama," Stewie sneered. "He wearin' ol' clothes, and his feet are covered with mud. He smells like fish."

"Hush now," Mrs. Pearson scolded. "You know Ida Mae's boy is always welcome at Sweet Kingdom Church no matter how he be dressed."

*Stewie's right for once*, thought Sugar. He hung his head, ashamed of his dirty bare feet, patched overalls, and wrinkled shirt. *What would Mama be thinkin', me lookin' like this comin' to church?*

Sugar heard singing. He looked up and saw Pastor Williams in his black Sunday suit. He was followed down the path between the chairs by the Sweet Kingdom Church choir, wearing scarlet robes trimmed with crisp white collars.

Behind the choir came the deaconesses in snowy white dresses and matching shoes.

Everybody stood and joined the choir, singing the old spiritual "Great Day! Great Day! The Righteous Marching, Great Day!" The procession made its way to the spot where a new shovel, a red ribbon tied to its handle, was stuck into the earth. The shovel marked the place where the new church would stand.

Pastor Williams stood behind the shovel and said a prayer about how anything could happen with hard work and the help of God. Then the pastor noticed Sugar sitting between Stewie and Mrs. Pearson.

"I see we have a special guest this mornin'," Pastor Williams said, pointing to Sugar. "Come on up here, James Earle." Necks craned to see Ida Mae's boy.

"Go on, Sugar," whispered Mrs. Pearson, nudging him out of his seat.

Stewie stuck out his foot. Sugar stumbled, barely keeping his balance. Stewie's sharp laugh rang in Sugar's ears. His face burned with embarrassment.

Paying no attention to Sugar's tattered appearance, Pastor Williams hugged the boy, then shook his hand. "This new church is gonna have a fine stain glass window 'cause your mama had a dream and worked hard for the window fund, son." Pastor Williams looked at the congregation. "I think it only fittin' that James Earle turn over the first shovelful of dirt to commemorate the buildin' of our new Sweet Kingdom Church."

Everyone jumped up and applauded as Sugar jammed the shovel into the earth with his bare foot and turned over a clump of dirt. As he made his way back to his seat, the choir led a rousing version of "This Little Light of Mine." Folks shook his hand and patted Sugar on his back as he passed. Never had he felt so proud.

"Swamp rat," Stewie hissed when Sugar sat down again. "You smell like dead fish. Phew! You stink." Stewie stuck out his tongue. Sugar ignored him. There was nothing Stewie could do or say that would spoil this moment for Sugar.

When the ceremony was over, Mama's friends came up and made a fuss over Sugar like he was a hero. Then it was time for the picnic. Church women set out platters of fried chicken, pots of baked beans, bowls of greens with chunks of ham, dishes of coleslaw, and jugs of lemonade and iced tea with fresh mint. Peach cobbler, concord grape jelly rolls, and pound cake were waiting for dessert.

After feasting on the wonderful food, Sugar joined the other children. Boys were playing tag, king of the mountain, and red rover. Some of the girls were chanting as they played hand-clapping games. Others sang jump rope rhymes.

It felt good to run around with children his own age, and Sugar lost all track of time. Before he knew it, the sun was slipping behind the grove of tall cottonwood trees lining the western edge of the cove. It was time to head back. Sugar knew Uncle Free would start to worry if he didn't return before the sun started to set.

Sugar made his way to where the great weeping willow hid his boat. He pushed it into the water, jumped in, and jammed the pole into the soft bottom of the cove. The small boat shot out from under the branches, startling the swarm of children who had run after him and were watching on the bank.

"Hey, Sugar," Stewie yelled after him. "You goin' back to that ol' swamp rat Free McBride?"

Ignoring the insult, Sugar thrust his pole

into the air and plunged it back into the water. The little boat surged ahead, leaving a rippling wake behind. Sugar noticed a breeze. Wind pickin' up, he thought.

From the bank a chorus of children's voices shouted, "Hey, can we have a ride?"

Sugar waved. "Sure," he yelled. "Someday."

Soon Sugar was out of the cove. He worked the pole until he was skimming into the deeper water of Sun Lake. He was standing tall, in control of his craft, like the captain of a ship.

A distant rumble caught Sugar's attention. Thunder? He studied the sky. Dark rain clouds were gathering quickly in the west. Knowing enough to get off the water at the first sign of a storm, he headed for the island in the middle of the lake.

# CHAPTER FOUR

**S**uddenly lightning pierced the dark clouds. The forceful wind slapped swirls of turbulent water against the boat. Sugar had to thrust his pole far into the water before it hit bottom.

*Too deep for polin'*, he thought. *I'd better jus' sit down and row.* Sugar grabbed the gunwales, stowed the pole, and slipped onto the seat of the rocking boat. He set the oars in the oarlocks, clasped the oars tightly, then rowed fast toward the island.

The sky became ominous. Rain began to fall in large drops, quickly drenching Sugar. Waves pounded the boat from every direction. It was all Sugar could do to hold on to the oars. *Ain't no time to be on the water*, he thought.

That morning neither Sugar nor Uncle Free had thought about the possibility of a sudden summer storm. Now rain was coming down in sheets. One capped wave after another lifted the small boat onto its crest, then pitched it down into the trough.

It was almost dark now. Lightning lit up the sky. Sugar was close to the north side of the island when he bumped up against something hard. By the time he saw the dense, muddy mass of branches, logs, and vines that barely broke the surface of the water, the waves had slammed his boat against it.

*A snag!* Sugar remembered Uncle Free's warning: "They be the most dangerous traps of all. Never, never let your boat get caught on a snag!"

Sugar jabbed one of his oars into the debris, trying frantically to work the boat free of the impenetrable tangle. *I'm stuck*, Sugar thought when the boat wouldn't budge. Desperately he tried to row clear of the treacherous snag. Then a huge wave bore down on him, snatching the oars from his hands and snapping them out of the oarlocks. The oars shot into the air like spears, then plunged into the water out of reach.

Grabbing the sides of the boat, Sugar braced himself. The next wave pressed the boat deeper into the snag. Sugar snatched the pole from under the seat and shoved.

Another swell jerked the pole from his hands and thrust it into the water. Sugar fell forward. He clutched the seat with both hands as the boat flipped over, pinning him underneath. It was pitch-black.

Sugar felt his legs pressed against the wall of mud and gnarled roots. Still clasping the seat, he lifted his head to discover a small pocket of air in the hull. He could breathe!

The water was icy cold. Sugar was afraid to let go, but he couldn't hang on much longer. He gulped a mouthful of air, then forced himself out from under the boat.

He was free! But now the waves were slapping him against the hull of the overturned boat. Sugar had to get away. He flipped onto his back, put his feet on the gunwale, and pushed himself clear. He grabbed a breath before another wave covered him, then turned onto his stomach and frantically dog-paddled into deeper water. The frothy swells swept him up and swirled him down like one of Uncle Free's cork fishing bobbers.

Sugar kept moving his arms and kicking his legs like Uncle Free had taught him. He found he could take quick little breaths between strokes of his arms. He was swimming, really swimming!

Slowly Sugar made his way toward shore. The rain let up and turned to a drizzle. The storm moved on. The sky cleared. The afterglow of the sunset was fading into dusk.

Sugar kicked and worked his arms until the water was just a few inches deep and his belly scraped the muddy bottom. He let the waves, almost gentle now, nudge him closer to the bank.

Finally Sugar dragged himself onto the shore and collapsed, exhausted.

After several minutes Sugar forced himself to stand. His legs wobbled. The boat! He stumbled along, searching. He could just make out the snag emerging from the water about fifty feet offshore, but there was no sign of his boat.

Sugar sank onto the soft bank. "Uncle Free gonna kill me," he moaned. "I busted his boat and almos' got myself drowned." Sugar lay down and sobbed. Softly he started moaning, "Uncle Free. Uncle Free . . ."

# CHAPTER FIVE

While Sugar was at the groundbreaking, Free had taken his own boat deep into the swamp to fish. After returning with a bucket of catfish, he gutted and skinned the fish on the porch cleaning table, then went inside to prepare a batter for frying them.

Free stopped before adding water and eggs to the mound of cornmeal he had poured into a bowl. "Best wait 'til Sugar gets back," he mumbled.

*Where that boy at?* Free thought, irritated.

*Groundbreakin' ceremony over long time ago. He don'
get home soon, I gotta go fetch him.*

Free went out onto the porch, lit his corncob
pipe, and limped to the edge of the dock. Not a
lot of sky was visible through the tall cypresses,
but the tips of the trees were swaying—a sign
the weather might be changing. Free knew how
fast a storm could blow up out of the west. He
peered into the swamp for a sign of Sugar.

Lightning shot through the sky. Then thunder
rumbled in the distance. Rain began to pour
down through the dense canopy of cypress trees.

Free snuffed out his pipe on the dock, untied
the rope of his boat, and jumped in. He shoved
off with a powerful thrust of his pole. Never
had he worked his pole so fast with his good
arm. Faster and faster the boat surged through
the swamp and into the bayou.

The wind picked up. Free had trouble keeping
the boat on course. He slipped onto the seat,
stashed the pole, and set the oars in place. His
weak arm always made rowing difficult, but with
great effort he worked the oars evenly. Soon Free
entered the more turbulent water of Sun Lake. *Hope
that boy had the sense to row for the island,* he thought.

The rain came full force on the wind. Free
was soon drenched and having trouble staying

on course as waves buffeted the boat. He could barely make out the island up ahead.

Almost as quickly as it had blown up, the storm passed. The rain turned to a steady drizzle and the waves died down. The sky cleared in the west, but the sun had already set and the evening was turning to dusk.

Free rowed to the south side of the island where he and Sugar practiced swimming. Free jumped out and shoved the boat onto the bank. He peered left and right, looking for signs of Sugar and his boat. Then Free realized Sugar probably tried to land on the north side of the island, the part closest to Cypress Grove. The snag! Free remembered he had never told Sugar about the snag on that side.

Free stumbled in the dim light as he made his way through the scrubby willow brush. "James Earle," he called loudly. "James Earle!"

Sugar jumped up when he heard Uncle Free's voice. "Uncle Free! Uncle Free!" he yelled. "Over here!" Waving his arms, Sugar scrambled to meet his uncle.

"Good Lord!" shouted Uncle Free. "What happened to you, boy?"

What a sight Sugar was, covered with mud and sand. Bits of brush and twigs were lodged in his hair. His overalls and shirt were in shreds. Blood lined the scratches on his forehead, arms, and legs.

"Uncle Free, I had an accident," Sugar sobbed. "The boat's gone. I almos' got myself drowned."

"It's all right," said Uncle Free. He knelt down and pressed the shaking boy to his chest with his good arm. "We can always build another boat, but there ain't no way to get another James Earle."

Sugar tried to tell what had happened, but Uncle Free just held him tight. "You can tell me 'bout it later," said Uncle Free. "We gotta get back home 'fore it gets dark. I didn' think to bring my lantern, and there ain't gonna be moonlight 'til later."

Together Uncle Free and Sugar shoved the boat into the water and swung it around so the bow faced the bayou. Sugar jumped in and knelt facing forward, like Uncle Free had taught him, so he could watch for submerged logs and those dangerous cypress knees. Free noticed that the boy was still shaking.

"Turn around, Sugar," Uncle Free told him. "I

reckon I know these waters good enough to get us home even as it's gettin' dark. Main thing is to clean you up and get that chill outta your bones."

Sugar carefully wiggled around to face his uncle.

"Okay," said Uncle Free. "Now's a good time to tell me why you didn' get home 'fore the sun start to set, like I thought you had the sense to do."

Sugar's words tumbled out. "I stayed too long at the picnic, but when I saw the sun goin' down, I hurried fast as I could. By the time I was on Sun Lake I heard thunder. Storm hit 'fore I could get to the island. Then waves smashed me into a snag. Water kept pushin' me against it. I lost my oars and pole. A wave flipped the boat over and I was trapped underneath."

"Whoa! Slow down," said Uncle Free, shaking his head. "What you mean you trapped under the boat?"

"It happened so fast, Uncle Free. All of a sudden I was hangin' on to the seat under the boat. Then I found this pocket of air in the hull. I could breathe!"

"Yeah, Sugar. I know there be air under an overturned boat. Jus' never thought to tell you.

Didn' think that somethin' you need to know right now. I'm grateful you learned it on your own 'fore it was too late. But how you manage to get out from under the boat and not get hung up on the snag?"

Sugar told his uncle what he did to get free—how he took a breath and plunged deep into the water to get loose of the boat, and how he swam clear of the snag and made it to shore.

"You a pretty smart boy for a ten year ol'," said Uncle Free.

"I'm eleven, goin' on twelve, Uncle Free," Sugar replied.

"You lucky to be goin' on twelve. You either got a good head on your shoulders or somebody lookin' out for you. Maybe both."

Sugar thought about what his uncle had said. "You ain't mad at me, Uncle Free? The boat's gone, and it's my fault."

"Prob'ly be good and mad at you in the mornin', boy," said Uncle Free. "And at myself too for not tellin' you 'bout the snag. But right now I'm jus' glad Ida Mae's boy safe and sound. We almos' home. I'm hungry and you mus' be starved. A mess of catfish waitin' to be fried."

Long dark shadows hung over the black

swamp water by the time Uncle Free eased the boat alongside the dock.

"Careful, boy, dock's slippery after the rain," Uncle Free warned. Sugar climbed out of the boat and looped the rope over the pier post. His legs felt a little stronger, and the quivering at the pit of his stomach was replaced with hunger pangs.

"You get washed up good, Sugar," said Uncle Free. "And you might as well pitch what's left of those clothes you wearin' into the rag bin."

Sugar went to the pump out back of the shack and scrubbed the sand and grit off his body with Uncle Free's homemade lye soap. The deep scratches on his face, arms, and legs smarted, but he could smell catfish frying. All he could think about was eating.

Sugar ran inside, slipped on clean overalls, and set the table while Uncle Free piled fried catfish and cornbread on a platter. Sugar shoveled the hot, tasty food into his mouth.

"Slow down, boy," said Uncle Free. "There's more where that come from."

"I ain't never been so hungry, Uncle Free," said Sugar, his mouth full.

"Hmm," Uncle Free replied. "So it seem."

After Sugar had eaten and the dishes had been cleaned and put away, Uncle Free lit a kerosene lantern and nodded for Sugar to follow him out onto the porch. They sat on the swing and gently swung back and forth. Uncle Free lit his corncob pipe. Blue smoke curled up toward the sky.

"Well, Sugar, maybe now you tell me somethin' 'bout the groundbreakin' ceremony. You did go, didn' you?"

"Sure I went," said Sugar. "But it seem like so long ago." Sugar sat silent for a few moments, recalling the day. Then he began to talk.

"Pastor Williams called me up in front of everybody. He ask me to dig the first shovelful of dirt in Mama's honor, and everybody clapped."

"Well, that be quite an honor, Sugar."

Sugar didn't say a word about Stewie Pearson calling him a swamp rat and talking bad about Uncle Free. He said nothing about being embarrassed because he hadn't dressed properly for the occasion, or how Mama's friends had fussed over him, wondering why she didn't send Sugar to live with them.

# CHAPTER SIX

I n the morning Uncle Free hunched over the stove making breakfast. He piled scrambled eggs and a mound of buttered grits on two plates and put a hunk of cornbread on top. This was Sugar's favorite breakfast.

"Come on, boy," said Uncle Free. "There ain't a minute to lose."

Sugar got up, pulled on his overalls, and walked over to the pump on the side of the sink to splash cold water on his face. Glancing out the window, Sugar saw mist rising from the water.

"Finish up, boy," Uncle Free said. "We gotta fetch that boat that got busted on the snag yesterday."

"But there ain't no more boat," said Sugar. "It broke apart and sank. Ain't nothin' left of it."

"Might be somethin' we can salvage. We gonna take a look. We can build a boat from a heap of scraps, if we can find 'em."

"NO!" said Sugar, upset. "I ain't goin'." Sugar's fear and hatred of the water welled up inside him.

"You stay with me, boy, you gonna need a boat," said Uncle Free. "Simple as that. We gonna go look for what's left of the one you smashed up."

Uncle Free was through arguing. He opened the screen door and walked across the porch onto the dock. He climbed into his boat. A long piece of coiled rope lay in the middle of it.

"I'm waitin' on you, boy!" Uncle Free hollered, pole in hand.

Sugar slammed the door behind him and ran to the boat, purposely rocking it as he jumped in. He sat down heavily in the bow and faced forward. Uncle Free almost lost his balance. He scowled at Sugar, then shoved off.

Sugar thought it was crazy to look for shreds of what might be left of his boat. He wanted nothing more to do with the swamp. He was tired of fishing day after day and sick of eating fish, frog legs, and turtle soup.

When they arrived at the island, Sugar hopped out and yanked the towrope hard to secure the boat. Uncle Free had to jump into the shallow water to avoid being tossed overboard. "Watch it, boy," he warned.

Uncle Free handed Sugar the coil of rope. "Carry this and follow me," Uncle Free commanded. Sugar looped his arm through the rope and trudged across the island after his uncle.

Soon they were on the bank where Sugar had first stumbled ashore. Studying the water, Uncle Free noticed a bar of sand and mud fifty feet offshore. It was covered with reeds and grasses.

"Hmm," Uncle Free said. "From the lake you don' see nothin' much of that big ol' snag. It's almos' completely underwater. You gotta know it's there. Ain't no wonder you smashed against it in the storm, boy. You lucky to get out from under when your boat flipped over."

Standing in the sunlight with the water glistening, Sugar's fear of the snag disappeared. It was hard to believe he'd been so terrified the night before.

From where they stood, there were no signs of Sugar's boat.

"I'm gonna swim over there and have a look," said Uncle Free. He waded into the water until it reached his chest, then dog-paddled to the sandbar. He stood up, ankle deep in the water.

About three inches below the surface, Free saw the hull of Sugar's overturned boat wedged against the muddy snag. The guide rope, attached to the iron ring on the bow, was tangled in the weeds. Uncle Free waved, then hollered to Sugar. "I see your boat. Bring the rope."

Sugar uncoiled the rope. At one end he made a loop, which he slipped over his shoulder. With the rope trailing behind him, he dog-paddled to where Uncle Free stood. There Sugar saw his boat. Amazingly, it was in one piece.

Uncle Free waded into deeper water. He fiddled with the guide rope but couldn't get it untied. Sugar watched as his uncle knotted the old rope and new one together.

"Don' know how bad it's lodged," Uncle Free called. He tried to tug the boat loose, but it wouldn't budge. "Gonna see if I can push it free from under the hull." Grabbing the sides, Uncle Free slipped under the boat. As he applied pressure the boat moved slightly.

Without thinking, Sugar dog-paddled to the deeper water. When his uncle resurfaced, Sugar was treading water next to him.

"Nothin' more we can do today," said Uncle Free. "We'll come back tomorrow with poles and iron grapplin' hooks to pry it loose. Boat ain't goin' anywhere."

"But the hull moved a little when you shoved it," Sugar said eagerly. "You pull the rope, Uncle Free. I'll go under and push against the mud wall with my legs like you was doin'."

Before Uncle Free could say no, Sugar dived under the boat. Breathing the air pocketed in the hull, he hung on to the seat for leverage. He pressed both feet against the snag and pushed as Uncle Free pulled from above. Slowly, the boat loosened from the mud and clutch of roots.

Sugar surfaced, blinked water out of his eyes, and shook his head to clear his ears. "Boat's loose, Uncle Free," he said. "Maybe we can tow it to the other side of the island now."

"Worth a try, boy, now that it's unstuck," said Uncle Free. "But first we gotta turn it over." Using all their strength, Sugar and Uncle Free rocked the boat until it finally turned right side up. Then Sugar swam to shore and ran through the brush across the island. He pushed Uncle Free's boat into the water and swiftly rowed to where his uncle waited on the sandbar. Uncle Free motioned for Sugar to row closer to the waterlogged boat.

"You think you can drag the boat to the other side by yourself?" Uncle Free asked as he tied the boats together.

"You ain't comin' with me?" said Sugar.

"Don' need two of us in the boat," said Uncle Free. "Make it too hard to row. Just take it nice and easy and row steady. It ain't far. I'll meet you across the island."

Sugar rowed slowly and carefully, towing the boat behind. As he approached the shore on the other side, Sugar jumped into the shallow water and untied his boat. Uncle Free waded over, and together they pushed the badly damaged boat onto land, then rolled it over so the hull could dry out.

"Ain't nothin' else we can do now, boy," said Uncle Free. "Let's give it three or four days to dry out good 'fore we take it home for repairs. It'll float then and not be so hard to pull."

"Okay," Sugar said, then added, "Uncle Free, I'll row back." Uncle Free nodded as they got into his boat. He sat in the bow, enjoying the ride to the shack.

There was little to eat in the kitchen except leftover cornbread. "Sugar, how 'bout you pick some slicing tomatoes from the garden," said Uncle Free. "Pull a couple onions while you're at it. I'll fry some potatoes. Then we can sit on the dock and maybe catch a fish or two. How 'bout it?"

"Sure, Uncle Free," Sugar replied. He grabbed a bucket and went out back, slamming the screen door behind him.

Later, waiting for fish to bite, Sugar and Uncle Free devoured the cornbread. Potatoes and onions were cooking slow in the covered iron fry pan, tomatoes were sliced.

"You did fine today, boy. Jus' fine," Uncle Free said.

"I'm sorry I was nasty to you this mornin'," said Sugar. "I was jus' scared 'bout goin' back out on the water."

"I know that, boy," said Uncle Free. "But I also know you had to get back there right away, otherwise those fears fester inside you. Hard to let 'em go. Somethin' bad happens, you gotta face it or the memories get buried deep inside and come out in strange ways later on. Don' forget that, boy."

Sugar knew Uncle Free was speaking the truth. It was the kind of thing Mama would have said.

# CHAPTER SEVEN

A*fter several days, Sugar and Uncle Free* went back to the island in Sun Lake. They towed the boat home, then set to overhauling it. Over the next three weeks they repaired the boat. Sugar was amazed at how much carpenter work his uncle could do with just one good arm.

"Get dressed," Uncle Free called to Sugar early one morning. "We gonna take your boat out to see if it floats." Sugar knew that was a joke. With the careful work they had done mending and sanding, the little boat looked like new.

Sugar threw back his quilt and pulled on his overalls. He grabbed a chunk of cornbread from the plate on the table, then ran into the yard where the boat was perched upside down on two wooden horses next to the shed. Sugar and Uncle Free carried it to the water and slid it in.

"Tighter than a drum," said Uncle Free. "Nary a drop of water seepin' in."

While his boat was being repaired, Sugar had been going along with Uncle Free to deliver frog legs, crawdads, catfish, crappie, and turtle meat to the folks in Cypress Grove. Now it was time for Sugar to start making the deliveries on his own.

The worst part of delivering fish in Cypress Grove was meeting up with Stewie Pearson, who never failed to yell "Hey, swamp rat!" when Sugar knocked on the Pearsons' door.

The best part of making deliveries was checking the progress on the new Sweet Kingdom Church building. Each time Sugar poled into the cove, he noted changes in the shape of the new church. Somehow this made him feel close to his mama. It was as if she were right there watching too, waiting for the day her stained glass window full of angels would fill the window hole.

When Sugar arrived back at the shack, Uncle Free would most likely be on the dock cleaning fish for their dinner. He'd chop off a fish's head, slit its underbelly, and run his thumb through the cavity, dropping the guts into a can. "Fresh food for the crawdads, boy," he'd say.

Sugar would take the can and dump the fish guts into the shallow swamp water. Then he'd go out back and dig up some potatoes, pick peppers, and pull a few onions. After shooing away the chickens, he would grab some eggs from the coop.

Inside, Sugar would light the stove. Without being told, he'd scoop cornmeal into the old crockery bowl, then add salt, eggs, and a little water to mix the batter for a batch of cornbread.

"New church comin' right along, Uncle Free," Sugar said one hot humid evening as they were eating their fried catfish, turtle soup, and Sugar's fresh-baked cornbread. "It's almos' all framed out."

"Hmm," said Uncle Free.

"Uncle Free, you know Mama started the stain glass window fund all by herself," said Sugar.

"Uh-huh," Uncle Free answered.

"You think money Mama saved from doin' laundry, and tips I got for deliverin' it, and money other folks gave gonna be enough to pay for the window?"

"Don' know nothin' 'bout how much a fancy window cost, James Earle," said Uncle Free, using Sugar's proper name. Sugar knew it was a signal Uncle Free didn't want to discuss his mama's window, but Sugar didn't let that stop him.

"Nobody else seem to feel a stain glass window very important," he went on. "But Mama said if you don' have some beauty in your life, what's the use of livin'."

Uncle Free sighed. "Your mama had beauty in her life. She saw it all around her. She the one taught me to look for beauty right here in the swamp. Like those yellow blossoms floatin' on the water. They called swamp lilies."

"Uncle Free," Sugar said, barely noticing the flowers. "I remember you and Mama arguin' a lot 'bout the window fund. You not the only one got mad at her for workin' so hard to get the money for it."

"Oh? Who else got mad at your mama?"

Uncle Free asked.

"Some of her friends, like Miz Pearson." Then, trying to sound like Stewie's mother, Sugar added, "Why you workin' your fingers to the bone for a special window, Ida Mae? Why we need a fancy colored glass window anyways?"

Sugar's imitation of Mrs. Pearson made Uncle Free chuckle. It reminded Sugar of how his uncle used to laugh with his mama while sitting around on the porch of their cabin.

# Chapter Eight

By the end of the summer Sugar was making all the fish deliveries to Uncle Free's customers in Cypress Grove. His rebuilt boat skimmed the water smoothly. It veered quickly to the left and right, depending on how Sugar manipulated his pole or moved the oars. *Either this boat is better than the ol' one or I'm gettin' better at steerin' it*, he thought.

"Roof's on!" Sugar shouted one day as he

poled into the cove of Cypress Grove and looked at the new church building. He eased his boat under the great willow tree and jumped out into the shallow water.

Sugar lifted the heavy wooden fish box out of the boat and set it carefully on the bank. Uncle Free's voice was always in his ear: "Watch you don' bruise the fish, and make sure you get 'em to the customers fast as you can, so they don' spoil."

After shoving his boat onto the bank, Sugar hitched the fish box over his shoulder, adjusting the wide leather strap to balance the weight. As he made his way up the hill, Sugar noticed something different about the church. "I didn' know the church gonna be brick," he said out loud.

Then Sugar noticed something else. The window hole at the front of the building was boarded up. "Why they board up the window?" Sugar asked himself. He knew from talking with Uncle Free's customers that Mama's window had already been commissioned from an art glass company in Memphis and would be delivered to the freight depot at the railroad station in Wilson City.

Sugar trudged up the dusty path. Melting ice seeped through the cracks in the fish box, dripping cold water down the legs of his overalls. It felt good in the heat.

Sugar's first customer was Mrs. Lucas.

"Didn' know the new church was gonna be brick, Miz Lucas," said Sugar, "Look mighty fine. Mama's stain glass window gonna look even more special framed by brick."

Mrs. Lucas gave Sugar a strange look but didn't say anything.

"Somethin' wrong with the fish, Miz Lucas? Uncle Free says to give you your money back if ever you don' think they good and fresh."

"Naw, Sugar, your fish the best there is. It ain't nothin', son, 'cept I heard it might take a little longer than planned to get the window in place."

"What you mean, Miz Lucas? The window break?" A sick feeling surged through Sugar.

"No, no, ain't nothin' like that, Sugar. I hear the window already been delivered to the freight depot."

Sugar was relieved. He grabbed the fish box and headed to his next customer to deliver some frog legs.

"I tell you, Sugar," said Miss Libby Louise, clicking her false teeth. "The argument 'tween the buildin' and the window committees almos' tore the church apart."

"Argument?" asked Sugar. "What argument?"

"Jus' some disagreement 'bout the way the money should be spent," Miss Libby Louise replied. "Don' you worry."

Sugar knew Mama wanted the window fund used for a stained glass window and nothing else, but he was too upset to ask any more questions. He slung the fish box over his shoulder and left without saying good-bye.

Down the road at Miss Manny's, Sugar carefully wrapped her turtle meat in old newspaper.

"Don' you fret none, Sugar. Maybe it be for the best—the deal the trustee board made for the brick," Miss Manny said, shaking her head. "I don' rightly know, myself."

"Beg your pardon, Miz Manny," said Sugar, "but I don' know nothin' 'bout a deal for buyin' brick."

"I jus' mean the stain glass window might not be in place for the dedication," Miss Manny explained. "That's all, Sugar. Don' you worry 'bout the window. It sure gonna get put in sometime or other."

By the time Sugar reached the Pearsons' house, his stomach was in knots. He knew something was terribly wrong. What was all this talk about church folks arguing and making deals for brick? Why wouldn't the stained glass window be put into the church if it was already delivered to the freight depot?

"Hey, swamp rat!" Stewie yelled from the steps of the porch. "Heard 'bout your mama's window?"

Before Sugar could answer, Mrs. Pearson stuck her head out the screen door and invited Sugar in. Sugar set down the fish box outside the door and picked out several cleaned catfish. He walked inside and put them on the lead sink.

"These are fine fish, Sugar," Mrs. Pearson said.

"Yes, ma'am. Uncle Free and I caught 'em this mornin'."

"Seems like you gettin' along jus' fine with your uncle" said Mr. Pearson. He was sitting at the kitchen table, sipping a glass of iced tea. "You learnin' the fishin' business. That's good and practical." Mr. Pearson ran the icehouse in Wilson City. Ever since he had come back to Cypress Grove to fish, Uncle Free had been getting his ice from Mr. Pearson.

Mrs. Pearson poured Sugar a glass of lemonade and motioned for him to have a seat.

"Thank you, Miz Pearson," Sugar replied. He wanted to be polite, but Mama's window was on his mind.

"Somethin's happened to Mama's window," Sugar said, the words tumbling out. "Why the window hole in the church all boarded up? Miz Manny say the stain glass window not gonna be in place for the church dedication. How come?"

Mr. Pearson cleared his throat. "Well, the truth is, son, the trustee board decided to borrow from the window fund to pay for the brick. Got a real good deal on it, and we felt we couldn' let an opportunity pass to build a brick church instead of a frame one. So it was decided to use plain glass 'til we can raise more money to pay for the stain glass window."

"Plain glass?" Sugar said, his voice starting to rise. "My mama worked for years for a stain glass window—not a plain one. Mr. Pearson, you head of the trustee board. How you let this happen?" Sugar was almost shouting.

"James Earle," Mr. Pearson said, trying to be patient. "Brick's a much more practical way to spend the money. But there ain't no need to worry, son. We already paid part of the money on ordering the window. When we build up the fund again, we can pay the rest and pick up the window from the freight depot. It called C.O.D.—cash on delivery. You pay your money and then you get what you ordered. Stationmaster in Wilson City's a friend of mine. He agreed to store the window free of charge 'til we raise the money."

"It took Mama years to raise money for that window." Sugar was near tears. "Ever since I remember, Mama was in charge of that window fund. Now all her hopes and dreams . . ." Sugar swallowed. "Gone!"

Mrs. Pearson reached out to Sugar. He backed away.

"Ida Mae was my best friend and all, but she was a dreamer," Mrs. Pearson said. "Sugar, you'll come to realize, jus' like all the other church members, that Mr. Pearson and the trustee board were right."

"NEVER!" yelled Sugar. "Y'all stole Mama's window money and bought bricks. You ain't nothin' but thieves!" He bolted out the screen door, slamming it behind him. Grabbing Uncle Free's fish box by the strap, Sugar ran across the porch.

Stewie had been listening from the top step of the porch. As Sugar raced out, Stewie stuck out his foot. Sugar went sprawling on his belly into the yard. The fish box hurtled into the air and came down with a thud, cracking. The fish flipped out onto the dusty ground.

"You mighty clumsy, Sugar," Stewie said with a nasty laugh. "Spoiled your fish too. Now you gotta repair that smelly ol' fish box."

Sugar was furious. He leaped to his feet, grabbed the tail of a catfish, and whacked Stewie across the face with it.

"AHHH! You little swamp rat," Stewie screamed. "You crazy jus' like your ol' broke-up uncle."

Mrs. Pearson charged through the screen door.

"You boys stop that fightin' right this minute, ya hear?" she shouted. But the boys were locked in a tangle of arms and legs as they tumbled in the dirt. Sugar whomped Stewie with the battered catfish every chance he got.

Mr. Pearson ran down the steps past his wife

and thrust the wrestling boys apart. Shoving Sugar back, he grabbed Stewie by the arm. "You get inside, son," he yelled. "And you get on home right now, James Earle," he told Sugar. "You be sure to tell your uncle Free exactly what happened. You don', I will!"

Mrs. Pearson stood with her arms on her hips, watching and hollering after Sugar. "Ida Mae would turn over in her grave to see you showin' out like this, boy!"

Sugar didn't answer or look back. He grabbed the cracked fish box and ran down the path. Scratches on his face, arms, and legs smarted. He ran past the houses of Uncle Free's customers. Some folks were on their porches or in their gardens. They looked up but didn't say anything as Sugar ran by. Without even glancing at it, he ran past the new Sweet Kingdom Church. All Sugar could think about was getting back to his boat. He ran to the cove and disappeared under the great willow.

Sugar stashed the fish box in the bow of the boat and climbed in. He felt sore all over. Catching his breath, he splashed his cuts with cool water and rubbed the places where he was bruised. He lay back, exhausted. Cradled in his little boat, Sugar fell asleep.

# Chapter Nine

**H**ours later Sugar woke up with a start to Uncle Free's sharp holler. "James Earle! James Earle, where you at?" It was almost dark. At first Sugar was afraid. His whole body ached. Then he remembered his fight with Stewie.

"Here, Uncle Free!" he shouted. "Under the willow."

The lantern secured to the tip of Uncle Free's boat bobbled as the bow parted the willow fronds. He poled next to Sugar's small boat. Even in the shadows Free could see that Sugar had been in a fight. His eye was swollen shut, and there was a gash on his cheek. "You a sorry sight, boy," he said.

"Uncle Free, I got in fight with Stewie Pearson, and, and . . ."

"Don' tell me nothin' 'bout what happened now," said Uncle Free, studying Sugar's bruises. "You feelin' up to followin' me home? It be pitch-dark soon."

"Sure, Uncle Free," Sugar said. He didn't complain about how he could barely see out of one eye. He concentrated on following Uncle Free's boat, taking care to stay in its gentle wake. Still, it was scary being on the water as it got darker and darker. Several lanterns Uncle Free had left burning on the dock served as beacons for the two boats making their way through the bayou into the swamp. Sugar shuddered at the thought he might have spent the night alone under the willow tree.

Uncle Free climbed onto the dock and secured his boat. He helped Sugar ease himself onto the pier. Sugar looped the guide rope over the post, then stored his oars and pole.

"You stay out here, Sugar," said Uncle Free. "I'll bring us some supper."

Sugar didn't argue. He plopped down and dangled his feet in the cool black water.

Uncle Free brought out a bucket of water, a rag, and a bar of lye soap and helped Sugar wash his face and hands. Sugar winced, but he didn't cry out. Then Uncle Free brought him a platter of cornbread and cold frog legs. He said nothing about Sugar's black eye, scratches, and torn overalls.

"Supper would've been hot had you been home on time," said Uncle Free, as he eased himself down on the dock next to Sugar. Sugar didn't respond. He was too busy eating. Uncle Free filled Sugar's plate twice and waited for him to finish.

"So how come I had to come huntin' you a second time in three months?" Uncle Free finally asked. "How come you got all tore up?"

The words tumbled out of Sugar. He told Uncle Free about the stained glass window and the bricks and how Stewie Pearson tripped him on purpose when he was delivering their fish.

"I fell off the steps into the yard. The fish box got cracked and the leftover catfish got pitched in the dust. I was so mad I grabbed a fish by the tail and whacked Stewie with it. That's when we started fightin'." Sugar took a deep breath. "Now there's no more Mama and no more stain glass window. Jus' gonna be a brick church with an ugly plain glass window."

"Hmm," said Uncle Free, absorbing Sugar's story. Then with a faint smile he added, "Tell me that part 'bout the catfish. How'd that go again?"

Forgetting his bruises, Sugar jumped up and replayed the fight in the shadowy light of the kerosene lanterns. Suddenly Uncle Free was there too. Holding his good arm in front of his face, Uncle Free shadowboxed with Sugar. The rickety dock rattled and shook as they wrestled, tussled, and poked each other in a mock fight.

Chuckling, Uncle Free limped over to the porch swing and collapsed onto the seat. Sugar sat on the floor beside him. "You danced around like a real boxer," said Sugar, catching his breath. "You ever box, Uncle Free?"

"A little, in Memphis, but I never told your mama. She never cotton to fightin', even the professional kind."

"Miz Pearson hollered at me," said Sugar. "She said Mama would turn over in her grave if she knew I was fightin'."

Uncle Free laughed. "Well, Miz Pearson got

that right." Then he was quiet, lost in thought. The silence amplified the swamp sounds and the creaking of the swing.

"You know what, Sugar," Uncle Free said after a while. "Maybe your mama not be mad after all. You was fightin' for your mama's window. Your mama knew some things worth you fightin' for." Uncle Free paused. "She might be right proud of you, son."

Sugar was thinking about Uncle Free's words when he noticed a yellow glow coming off the water. "What's that, Uncle Free?" he whispered.

"Some folks call it will-o'-the-wisp. Some call it jacky-lantern. It ain't nothin' but the glow of swamp gases," said Uncle Free.

"Oh," said Sugar, accepting Uncle Free's explanation of yet another swamp mystery. He and Uncle Free sat and listened to the night music. The high-pitched clacking of cricket frogs harmonizing with the deep drumming of the bullfrogs no longer sounded strange to Sugar.

Fireflies flickered on and off over the black water lapping against the pier. June bugs bombarded hundreds of swarming moths drawn toward the lantern lights. For the first time since he had come to live with Uncle Free, Sugar started to feel at home.

# CHAPTER TEN

In the morning Uncle Free was up before dawn. He shook Sugar.

"Wake up, Sugar!" Uncle Free said, bending over him. "I gotta go up to Wilson City today. I'll be home after dark."

Now and again Free went to Wilson City to get coffee, flour, and sugar, and to stop at the bank to deposit the money he and Sugar had earned from selling fish.

"Can I come too?" Sugar asked. He never liked staying in the swamp by himself. "I can help."

"Not today, Sugar," said Uncle Free. "I be goin' alone this time."

"What am I gonna do all day by myself?" asked Sugar, feeling a little left out. "Ain't no fish orders to deliver for a day or two."

"Same as we do together," said Uncle Free. "You gonna fish. Only today you do it by yourself. And you might spend some time in the shed patchin' the fish box. Mighty big crack you put in it yesterday."

Then Uncle Free was gone. Sugar got up and pulled his quilt up over his cot. He put on a fresh pair of overalls, made himself some breakfast, then cleaned the dishes. By the time Sugar had fished and worked on fixing the wooden fish box, the day was almost gone. He made himself some supper and went out on the porch as the sun went down.

Sugar was amazed at how peaceful it was and how the dark shadows cast by the tall, lacy cypress trees didn't scare him anymore. He was surprised to realize he had enjoyed his day alone in the swamp. Wonder if Mama knew I would come to like livin' here with Uncle Free, Sugar thought.

Naw, how could she?

Sugar yawned and decided to go to bed early. He lit the porch lantern to help guide Uncle Free to the dock.

By the time Free returned later that evening, Sugar was asleep, curled up in his quilt. "Snug as a bug in a rug," Free said softly, recalling what Ida Mae often whispered to Sugar. Free suddenly missed his sister. Hope she think I be doin' a good job with her boy, he thought.

Free noticed Sugar had left him a bowl of grits, a mess of pan-fried catfish, and a plate of steamed crawdads for his supper. The mended fish box was set neatly on a stool. Free smiled. I reckon Ida Mae be pleased, he thought. But ain't so much my doin'. Ida Mae the one who raised him right.

During the next week, Sugar and Uncle Free spent their days fishing, catching turtles, gigging for frogs, and mending their nets. Sugar realized so many things about the swamp—like the snakes slithering in and out of the lilies growing in the shallow water—no longer scared him.

When Sunday came, Sugar rose early and after breakfast began clearing the dishes. That's when he noticed Uncle Free was standing in front of the mirror next to the sink, shaving. He had on a clean undershirt and a new pair of pants. His suspenders were hanging down over his hips as he carefully guided the razor over his face. Sugar saw Uncle Free had polished his best pair of shoes too.

Sugar hadn't seen his uncle so dressed up since Mama's funeral.

"They dedicatin' the new church today," said Uncle Free. "Ain't you goin'?" His voice was almost cheerful.

"Gotta work, Uncle Free," said Sugar. "You the one always tellin' me if we don' work, we don' eat." He picked up a fishnet and sat on his cot twisting and weaving the strands to repair the tears.

"I think your mama would want us to go," said Uncle Free.

"Us go?" replied Sugar. "Church folks ain't your kinda folks, remember? Now they ain't my kind either. And there ain't gonna be no stain glass window, so why bother goin' to the dedication?"

"I think your mama would want us both to be there," Uncle Free insisted. "Window or no window."

Sugar didn't respond. Free glanced at him in the reflection of the mirror. Sugar's head was down and his eyes were intent on mending the net in his hands.

Uncle Free patted his face dry, put on the new shirt hanging on the back of the chair, and pulled up his suspenders. Then he went over to the cupboard and pulled out a box. "Want you to open this up, James Earle," Uncle Free said, setting the box on the table.

Curious, Sugar put down the net. RAYMOND'S DRY GOODS, WILSON CITY was printed on the side of the box. Sugar took off the lid and there, folded neatly, were a new white shirt, brown pants, black shoes, socks, underwear—a whole new set of clothes.

"Why you buy me new clothes?" Sugar asked. "I got a clean, pressed shirt and pants in the dresser from Mama's funeral."

Uncle Free went over to the old dresser and pulled out Sugar's Sunday clothes. "You wanna wear these, go ahead."

Sugar slipped on the shirt. The sleeves were

inches too short. He held up the pants. They barely came to his ankles.

"I guess I grew," Sugar said sullenly. "But that ain't no reason to get new Sunday clothes. Ain't no place to wear 'em 'cept church, and I don' go there anymore. Jus' like you."

Sugar stomped across the room. "So that's why you went to Wilson City—to buy me new clothes for the church dedication?"

"Somethin' like that," said Uncle Free.

"Why you wanna go to the dedication anyways, Uncle Free? You the one said Mama was foolish workin' so hard and givin' her money for a stain glass window." Sugar was angry now. "I ain't goin' to see somethin' dedicated when it ain't even there."

"Maybe we wrong," said Uncle Free. "Maybe the trustee board be right. Maybe your mama would agree a brick church more important than a stain glass window."

Uncle Free turned to go. "You do what you like, James Earle. Me, I'm goin' to the dedication."

Slamming the screen door behind him, Uncle Free limped down the dock, untied his boat and climbed in. With a shove of his pole, he headed toward Cypress Grove.

Sugar ran to the edge of the dock. "Mama didn' want no brick church," he hollered. "She want the stain glass window be in place for the dedication. I KNOW she did."

Uncle Free moved swiftly through the water. He didn't answer or turn around.

# CHAPTER ELEVEN

**F**urious at the church folks and mad at his uncle, Sugar stood on the dock and watched Uncle Free pole out of the swamp into the bayou. Then Sugar stormed back inside. He plopped down on his cot and began picking at the frayed fishnet.

After a few minutes Sugar got up and looked inside the box of clothes. *Clothes jus' like Mama would've bought for Christmas or Easter,* he thought.

Tears filled his eyes. With a sudden sweep of his arm, Sugar flung the box on the floor. Shirt, pants, shoes, socks, and underwear went flying. He collapsed onto his cot and wept.

"You actin' like a baby," Sugar said to himself as his sobbing subsided. "Jus' feelin' sorry for yourself." He picked up the clothes from the floor and laid them out on the cot. Then he walked over to the old lead sink, took off his overalls, and began pumping icy spring water over his head.

"Whew!" Sugar said, shivering. He scrubbed his hair, face, ears, neck, and arms with Uncle Free's lye soap. He rubbed himself dry in a hurry to get warm.

Quickly Sugar put on his new underwear, shirt, and pants. He glanced in the mirror as he brushed his hair. Uncle Free had insisted on trimming Sugar's hair a few days ago.

"Why you gotta mess with my hair," Sugar had complained. "Nobody care how long it gets."

"I care," Uncle Free had said.

"So that's why Uncle Free wanna cut my hair," Sugar said. "So it look nice for the dedication."

Sugar grabbed his new shoes, stuffing the

socks into the toes as he ran out the door. He placed the shoes in the bow of his boat where they wouldn't get wet. Swiftly he untied the boat from the dock and climbed into the stern. He shoved off with his pole, careful not to splash water on his new clothes.

Sugar wasn't sure why he was all dressed up, hurrying toward Cypress Grove. He didn't want to go to the dedication of the new Sweet Kingdom Church. Conflicting emotions bubbled up inside him. Nevertheless, he poled forward quickly and smoothly.

As he approached Cypress Grove, Sugar could see the new brick church nestled among the trees. Maybe Uncle Free be right, thinkin' Mama might agree with the trustee committee, Sugar thought.

Rounding the bend, Sugar saw the crowd gathered near the shoreline of Sun Lake. They were getting ready to parade up the path into the church for the sermon and singing part of the ceremony.

Nobody seemed to notice Sugar enter the cove and slip under the weeping willow branches. He poled alongside Uncle Free's boat and rolled up his pant legs so they wouldn't get wet when he stepped into the shallow water. He pulled the bow of his boat onto the grass, adjusted his clothes, and put on his new socks and shoes.

"Ouch!" Sugar said when he stood up. "Uncle Free got everythin' right 'cept these shoes. They too tight."

Sugar watched the procession of folks in their Sunday best from behind the canopy of willow fronds. *At least I be dressed like Mama would have wanted, IF I was goin' to the dedication,* he thought. *Which I ain't.*

Pastor Williams led the way, followed by the choir, dressed in their flowing scarlet robes, singing "Walking Up the King's Highway." *Mama's favorite hymn,* thought Sugar.

Then came the church members, singing along with the choir. Girls in starched, ruffled frocks, white socks, and Sunday shoes and boys in pressed pants and shirts and freshly shined shoes marched proudly with their parents. Bringing up the rear was Mr. Pearson and the trustee board members, followed by Mrs. Pearson with Stewie in tow.

Sugar noticed Uncle Free was lagging behind, limping along slowly but looking good in his new store-bought clothes in spite of his bent body. *Uncle Free ain't no swamp rat*, he thought. *No matter what Stewie Pearson say.*

Sugar watched the last of the congregation enter the church before he shot out from under the willow branches and raced up the path. He rushed past his uncle, around toward the front of the church where the stained glass window should have been.

Impulsively Sugar reached down and grabbed a rock. His new shoes pinched, but he barely noticed. He thrust back his arm and aimed at the center of the window.

Then abruptly Sugar dropped the rock. He spun around and almost crashed into Uncle Free, who had run after him, bad leg and all. Uncle Free grabbed Sugar with his good arm.

"It was Mama," Sugar sobbed, pressing his face against Uncle Free's shoulder. "I wanted to break that plain glass window, but Mama wouldn't let me do it."

Uncle Free held the trembling boy close. "That don' surprise me, son," Uncle Free said. "I told you she jus' might want you to go to the dedication, not to wreck the church window, even a plain glass one."

Uncle Free pulled his handkerchief from his

pocket and wiped Sugar's face. "I see you did a good job washin' up, but now your face all stain with tears," said Uncle Free, examining Sugar. "New clothes fit nice. Look good too. Let's go on inside."

"But, Uncle Free, I don' wanna go to the dedication. Can' we jus' go back home?" Sugar pleaded. "Please."

Uncle Free gently but firmly grabbed Sugar's arm and led him toward the front door to the church. "Sometimes we gotta do things we don' wanna do, James Earle. This here's one of them times." There was no arguing with Uncle Free when he spoke in that tone of voice.

Sugar and Uncle Free entered through the heavy oak doors that framed the entrance to the new Sweet Kingdom Church. The choir and congregation were harmonizing on the last stanza of "Great Day! Great Day! The Righteous Marching, Great Day!"

# CHAPTER TWELVE

Pastor Wilson looked up from the freshly varnished pulpit and saw Free McBride and Sugar standing behind the last pew. He beckoned them to come down front. Sugar, staring at the black curtain in front of the window, was frozen in his spot.

Uncle Free squeezed Sugar's arm and nudged him to move, but Sugar resisted and tried to pull away. Uncle Free bent down and whispered, "James Earle, we goin' to the front of the church. I know you don' wanna, but you ain't got no choice."

There was no breaking away from Uncle Free. Together they made their way down the aisle.

"Swamp rats!" hissed Stewie, wedged between his mama and daddy.

"Hush, boy!" Mr. Pearson's voice was as sharp as a viper's tongue.

Uncle Free pressed his fingers around Sugar's arm. "Ignore that, son," he whispered. Sugar didn't turn around. He kept walking as if in a trance.

There were two empty chairs in the front row where the deacons sat. Pastor Williams gestured them to the seats of honor. Sugar didn't feel like being honored. All he wanted was to escape back to Uncle Free's shack in the swamp.

*Stewie's right,* Sugar thought, *I'm a swamp rat. I don' deserve to be in a fancy church like this. Maybe when Mama was alive, but no more. It don' matter that I'm wearin' nice new clothes. I'm nothin' but a swamp rat like Uncle Free.*

Sugar was so deep in thought, he barely heard Pastor Williams's sermon, which was about understanding and loving one another and the importance of having dreams.

Then the pastor called Mr. Pearson to come forward to say a few words. Making his way to the pulpit, he cast a friendly look in Sugar's direction. Sugar turned away, not wanting to face Mr. Pearson.

"James Earle," said Mr. Pearson, looking directly at Sugar. "Your mama, Ida Mae Martin, had a dream."

*Yeah*, thought Sugar, *and y'all stole it!* He stared up at the black curtain draped in front of where Mama's window should have been.

"But it was Ida Mae's son, James Earle, who kept his mama's dream for a stain glass window alive when the rest of us lost sight of it," Mr. Pearson went on. "James Earle, would you please step up here?"

*What's all this talk 'bout dreams*, Sugar was thinking when Uncle Free nudged him. "Get up, son," whispered Uncle Free. "Mr. Pearson callin' you up to the front." Feeling numb, Sugar walked toward the pulpit.

"James Earle," said Mr. Pearson, "would you please pull this cord?"

Pastor Williams put a thin rope in Sugar's palm. It was attached to the black curtain on a pulley. Mr. Pearson and Pastor Williams nodded, and Sugar tugged.

Suddenly the curtain fell to the floor, revealing a window with the sun shining through red, pink, purple, green, yellow, and blue stained glass. Black angels floated up and down a shimmering staircase that reached into a heaven of blue and white clouds.

There were gasps from the congregation as folks jumped to their feet and burst into applause. Sugar couldn't take his eyes off the beautiful window. Stumbling, he returned to his seat next to Uncle Free.

When folks settled down, Mr. Pearson continued. Sugar was barely listening.

"It was James Earle's faith in Ida Mae's dream, with some help from an anonymous donor, that led to the stain glass window bein' installed in time for this dedication," said Mr. Pearson.

Sugar jolted to attention. Anonymous donor? *Who that be?* he wondered. *And why they wanna keep it a secret?*

"The trustee board knew what was best for our physical well-bein' by buildin' a church outta brick," said Mr. Pearson. "But it was Ida Mae who knew what was best for our souls. James Earle knew it too. James Earle was even willin' to fight for it." Then Mr. Pearson led the congregation in a fresh round of applause sprinkled with loud, joyous shouts of "Amen," "Glory Be," and "Praise the Lord."

Pastor Williams nodded, and the choir started to sing "Glory Alleluia! A Great Day Is A-Coming." The congregation began to chant the Amen chorus. All Sugar could do was sit there staring at Mama's window.

Before he knew it, Sugar was swept outside onto the lawn with Uncle Free and folks from the congregation. Church women served everyone platters of fried chicken, barbecued ribs, greens, potato salad, coleslaw, baked beans, watermelon slices, fresh apple pies, and jugs of lemonade and iced tea. Mama's old friends fussed over Sugar as if he was some kind of hero.

While the grown-ups visited, the children ran off and played statues and tag. Sugar joined them. Stewie hung back.

"Hey, Stewie," Sugar hollered. "Come on."

Reluctantly Stewie entered into the games. Sugar acted as if nothing bad had happened between them. He knew this was not a time to hold a grudge.

Now and again Sugar heard Uncle Free's laugh above the din of the crowd. It reminded Sugar of how Uncle Free and Mama used to laugh together.

Finally Uncle Free came over and called to Sugar, "We gotta get back 'fore dark, son." They pulled themselves away from the crowd and waved good-bye.

"Hey, Sugar," one of the children called after them. "You promised us a ride in your boat."

"Someday soon," Sugar called back.

Uncle Free and Sugar slipped under the great weeping willow. They removed their shoes and socks, waded into the shallow water, and hopped into their boats.

Sugar led the way across Sun Lake. As he maneuvered into the bayou, Sugar shouted, "Look, Uncle Free! Swamp vine bloomin' there on that cypress tree."

"So it is, Sugar," called Uncle Free. "You noticin' all sort of things you never paid no mind to 'fore now."

It was true. Sugar pointed to a great blue heron daintily tiptoeing along the edge of the water. Then he looked up, and through the canopy of cypresses he saw an eagle circling high above. Sugar also noticed how the sun shining through the overhanging mosses made delicate patterns on the water and how the water sparkled in the dappled light.

Sugar rowed along in silence. After a while he called out, "Uncle Free! There's somethin' else I noticed. You seem to know all 'bout the stain glass window bein' in place for the dedication."

"Well," said Uncle Free. "I know what you know. Some anonymous donor pay for the window so it be put in the church. That's all there was to it."

"That ain't all there was to it, and you know it."

"Maybe somebody jus' want it to be a secret," said Uncle Free.

"That somebody be you!" Sugar exclaimed.

Uncle Free didn't say a word.

"Mama knew jus' what she was doin' when she sent me to live with you, didn' she, Uncle Free?" said Sugar.

"She sure did, son. She knew exactly what she was doin'. Lots more than I knew what she was doin'." Uncle Free let out a laugh that echoed all the way to Cypress Grove. Sugar laughed too, sounding just like Uncle Free.

As the sun set over the swamp, the shack came into view. "We almos' there, Uncle Free," said Sugar. "We almos' home."

# AFTERWORD

Owen Whitfield (1894–1965) was a sharecropper, working in poverty on a farm owned by someone else. He was also an ordained minister and a civil rights activist whose heroic work on behalf of farm laborers was documented in the film *Oh Freedom After While: The Missouri Sharecropper Protest of 1939*. Lynn Rubright, the author of this book, was a coproducer of the documentary.

Right now you are probably asking yourself, "What do Owen Whitfield and a documentary about a labor leader have to do with *Mama's Window*?" Actually, the fictional story told in *Mama's Window* was inspired by episodes in the early life of Owen Whitfield, and Sugar is loosely based on Whitfield as a boy. "While researching the adult life of Whitfield," says Rubright, "I found a profile of him by Fannie Cook, a writer whose papers are housed at the Missouri Historical Society. These papers gave a few details about Whitfield's childhood. Fourteen years later, this book is the result of that discovery."

Owen Whitfield was born on a Mississippi plantation called The Eagle's Nest. Although his family lived in poverty, they valued hard work, high morals, and education. Whitfield's mother washed clothes in a spring and ironed in the open, and young Owen delivered the clean laundry to her customers. The pennies, nickels, and dimes they earned went toward his mother's pledge for a window for their church." Unfortunately, his mother died before the window was in place.

To be certain her story reflected the appropriate setting, time, and place, Rubright made several trips to Mississippi and consulted with numerous authorities about life in the region. From one of Fannie Cook's stories generously provided by her son, Howard, Rubright learned about the childhood experiences that helped shape Whitfield's adult attitudes.

Reverend Dr. Martin Luther King, Jr. was not the first African American leader to use a nonviolent approach to social change. In 1939 Reverend Whitfield organized and directed a sharecropper's strike involving more than fifteen hundred black and white families. He called for the farm workers to abandon their rickety shacks and "live out in the weather" to show their solidarity against the oppressive sharecropping system.

This was particularly remarkable since at the

time many states in the southern United States were segregated. Blacks and whites did not go to school together, live in the same neighborhoods, or eat in the same restaurants. Whitfield organized black and white sharecroppers using their shared poverty as a rallying point. He convinced them to set aside racial differences and work together for the good of the entire community.

In response to Whitfield's call to action, the protestors pitched tents along highways 60 and 61 in southeast Missouri. For days the strikers endured bitterly cold weather and continual harassment by the landowners. Observers waited for the protestors' will to break, but it never did.

During the strike, Whitfield's life was threatened—many times. Still he would not give up. His strength gave the demonstrators courage, and they remained on the roadside until they forcibly were hauled away in trucks by state police.

Some whites accepted a black man's leadership, but the integrated movement angered the Ku Klux Klan, a white supremacist organization, and other anti-civil rights groups. They resented Whitfield's position and plotted to kill him. Reluctantly leaving his family and followers in the Missouri bootheel, Reverend Whitfield fled to St. Louis. There he met Fannie Cook, a social worker, who immediately offered to help by introducing him to several influential people. At a meeting in Cook's home, the Committee for the Rehabilitation of the Sharecropper was formed to champion the sharecroppers' cause.

Thereafter, Whitfield, his wife, Zella, and Fannie Cook became colleagues in the struggle for economic justice for blacks. Their uncommon friendship, based on honesty and mutual respect, lasted for many years, through good times and bad.

The little boy who would not allow his spirit to be maimed by anger became a man who truly understood the meaning of peace, forgiveness, and love. He was respected and admired for his compelling oratory and revered for his genius at organizing. Whether Whitfield was addressing his rural Baptist congregation, discussing union matters with Southern Tenant Farmers' Union (STFU) or Congress of Industrial Organizations (CIO) officials, or conversing with President Franklin D. Roosevelt and first lady Eleanor Roosevelt at the White House, he remained steadfastly committed to God, his family, and his people. — *Patricia C. McKissack*

# Author's Note

Patricia McKissack and I have been friends since she taught eighth-grade English to my son thirty years ago. After she left teaching to become an editor and author, Pat edited my first book, *For the Bible Tells Me So, Bible Story-Plays with Puppets,* which I co-wrote with Ruthilde Kronberg and Louise Ulmer.

Our friendship deepened when Pat, working on her master's degree in teaching at Webster University, St. Louis, Missouri, became a student in my Storytelling Across the Curriculum course. It was exciting to watch Pat discover how she could bring her written stories dramatically to life orally. Years later, Pat told me that the idea for her book *Flossie and the Fox* grew out of my storytelling course. "My grandfather told us kids stories on the front porch in Nashville, Tennessee," she said. "Your course helped me realize that life experiences and memories are great foundations for fictional stories, but nonfiction can be equally as exciting to tell and write."

If my storytelling course helped Pat discover the power of her voice in spoken word, she in turn has become my mentor and helped me develop immeasurably as a writer. She encouraged my extensive research for *Mama's Window*, which was inspired by a draft of a short story written by Fannie Cook around 1940. Pat and her husband, Fred, helped me learn about and appreciate the richness and complexity of African American music, culture, heritage, and history.

Pat and I are both active in the National Storytelling Network and National Council of Teachers of English, where we each have presented programs on storytelling, literacy, and writing processes. During frequent St. Louis family get-togethers, we celebrate our love and respect for each other and our children and grandchildren, and of course indulge our mutual passion for story. —*Lynn Rubright*

# ACKNOWLEDGEMENTS

Special thanks to Patricia and Fredrick McKissack, authors and historians, for the guidance, honesty, and encouragement without which *Mama's Window* could not have been written; and to Philip Lee and Louise May, wise and insightful editors at Lee & Low Books.

Thanks also to the following people for their help in making *Mama's Window* a reality: Howard Cook, Evanston, Illinois, son of Fannie Cook, who shared memories of his mother's friendship with Owen Whitfield as well as a draft of one of her stories, which was the inspiration for this book; ministers Shirley Whitfield Farmer and Clay Farmer, St. Louis, Missouri, daughter and son-in-law of Owen Whitfield, for their continued love and support; John Fewkes, cultural historian, Dundee, Mississippi, for sharing his knowledge of traditional folkways; John Ruskey, Clarksdale, Mississippi, Delta blues musician, canoe builder, artist, and river man, who took me on the rivers, bayous, and swamps; Reverend John Polk, for sharing his stories of growing up in the Delta; Christopher Gordon, associate archivist, Missouri Historical Society, St.

Louis, fisherman and historian, who helped with the research; Ellen Eliceiri, head of Reference Services and Collection Development, Emerson Library, Webster University, St. Louis, Missouri, for her faith in this project; Soozi Williams, assistant director, Marked Tree Delta Area Museum, Marked Tree, Arkansas, and her husband, Tom, for sharing stories about "grabbin'" catfish by hand; and Mary Gay Shipley, owner of That Book Store, Blytheville, Arkansas, who led me to Brian Baudis, refuge manager, Big Lake National Wildlife Refuge, Manila, Arkansas.

I also appreciate the help from Leigh McWhite, Archives and Special Collections, University of Mississippi (Oxford); Kay Newman and Richard Taylor, Tunica Museum, Tunica, Mississippi; Jim Price, archeologist, Ozark National Scenic Waterways, Van Buren, Missouri; Frank Nickell, director, Center for Regional History, Southeast Missouri State University, Cape Girardeau; John Warren Stewig, author and director of the Center for Children's Literature, Carthage College, Kenosha, Wisconsin; Ann Morris, former director, Western Historical Manuscript Collection, University of Missouri, St. Louis; Jean Streeter Cadle, former archivist of Fannie Cook Papers, Missouri Historical Society,

St. Louis; Marilyn Dulaney and Doris Frazier, St. Louis gospel singers; and Arthur Toney, Music Minister, St. Peter's African Methodist Episcopal Church, St. Louis, Missouri.

Thanks for continued words of encouragement from Annette Harrison and Ruthilde Kronberg, master storytellers, Constance Levy, poet, and June Von Weise, master teacher, St. Louis, Missouri; Marlene Birkman, professor, School of Education, Webster University, St. Louis, Missouri; Dick Bradley, Milwaukee, Wisconsin; Sara Larsen, Sister Bay, Wisconsin; and Meg Peterson, writer-playwright, Maplewood, New Jersey. —*Lynn Rubright*